THE REVOLTING RABBLES

Bringing the past to life, warts and all!

Ruffs and Ruffians

SUSAN GATES

Illustrated by Leo Broadley

Scholastic Children's Books,
Commonwealth House, 1-19 New Oxford Street,
London, WC1A 1NU, UK
a division of Scholastic Ltd
London ~ New York ~ Toronto ~ Sydney ~ Auckland
Mexico City ~ New Delhi ~ Hong Kong

First published in the UK by Scholastic Ltd, 2002

Text copyright © Susan Gates, 2002

Cover and inside illustrations copyright © Leo Broadley, 2002

ISBN 0 439 99601 5

Typeset by M Rules
Printed by Cox & Wyman Ltd, Reading, Berks.

10 9 8 7 6 5 4 3 2 1

Ruffs and Ruffians

Two cries of distress from somewhere in the café tell me what's happened to Ryan's and Rupert's yoghurt. It's gone catapulting through the air and bombed some poor people. Quite a lot of people really. Everyone seems to be wiping it off their clothes, out of their hair. It's all over the place. How can two spoonfuls of yoghurt splatter so far?

"Where's your ruff spoon?" I shout at Ryan.

"Er, I couldn't hold on to it. It's escaped. It's over there somewhere."

Oh no! It's writhing on the floor between tables. There's a woman trying to stamp it to death.

Look out for more books in this revolting
series. . .

Boils and Blisters
Toffs and Toshers

To my own rabble of a family –
Laura, Alex, Chris and Phil.

Chapter One

"So what do we have to do at this Elizabethan Fayre, Dad?"

"Oh, just stroll through the crowds in our costumes," Dad tells me. "You know, 'Make History Come Alive'."

"Can I be Queen Elizabeth?" I ask him.

"You don't want to be her," says my little brother, Rupert. "She tried to ban football."

1

"Oh, go on, Dad. Let me be someone rich and famous for once. I'm sick of being a humble peasant."

"Of course you can't be Queen Elizabeth, Rae," says Dad in a hurt voice, as if I've let him down. "I'm surprised you even asked! Remember the principles of Rent-a-Rabble. We never do kings and queens."

"Yeah, right, Dad," I groan.

I wish I'd never brought it up. Because it's got Dad on his soap-box. Rent-a-Rabble is Dad's personal mission. He gets really worked up about it.

"We at Rent-a-Rabble play the people that time forgot. The invisible people. The ragged and wretched who never got dealt a lucky hand. We show the dirt, the grime, the festering sores, the gritty bits of history!"

"Richard!" Mum reminds my dad sharply. "Please! This is breakfast-time."

Reluctantly Dad shuts up. He carries on crunching his toast.

But Rupert takes over, spraying out toast crumbs. It would take more than Mum to shut him up. Mum's far too polite. You have to threaten Rupert with Death. But even if you say, "Shut up or die!", you can see that he finds it a really tough choice.

"Can I be a swineherd, Dad, can I, can I?" begs Rupert, greasing round Dad as usual.

"Creep!" I mouth at him. But he pretends not to notice.

Ever since we were medieval peasants on our last job, and he got friendly with a pig called Gilbert, it's been Rupert's ambition to be a swineherd. That makes my dad really proud. Other dads want their kids to be lawyers or brain surgeons. But you've probably noticed that my dad's different.

"Actually," says Dad, giving a quick glance at Mum before he dares open his mouth, "it's funny you should say that, Rupert. But I bought this brilliant book in a second-hand bookshop about Elizabethan fayres. And there were loads of humble, downtrodden folk at them. This job is right up Rent-a-Rabble's street."

I ought to explain. I'm Rae Rabble. And I'm in Rent-a-Rabble. That's our family firm. We hire ourselves out for historical events.

"And talking of pigs," says Dad, "there's a

3

description of a poor lady swineherd in my book." Dad quotes from memory. "*Verily, she was a whale of a pig woman with a mangy face and foul breath that reekt of the pigsty.*"

"Nope," I say before he can ask me. "I am not being that pig woman. Clear?"

"I'll be a pig woman, Dad," smarms Rupert, "Please let me, Dad, please, please, please. I'd be a brilliant pig woman!"

I kick him under the table.

"What about a Bearded Lady?" Dad asks me. "Poor, unfortunate folk like that were often displayed as freaks at Elizabethan fayres."

"No way!" I tell him. "Are you joking? My friends might be there."

But, what a surprise, Rupert says, like a shot, "Let me be a Bearded Lady!"

Dad gives me a disappointed look.

"Sometimes, Rae," he says, sadly, "I don't think you're one hundred per cent committed to the principles of Rent-a-Rabble."

"Yes, I am. I just don't want to look like a total idiot, that's all!"

I've got to live in the twenty-first century.

That's not Dad's problem. He seems to live permanently in the past. What can you expect? Before he got made redundant and started Rent-a-Rabble, he worked at the History Museum for years and years.

Rupert's pawing at Dad's shoulder. "What can I be then, Dad?"

"How about a pathetic, starving vagabond, son?" suggests Dad. "*Rascally rabble and riff-raff*, it calls them in my book. But they were really poor folk, forced to beg and steal to survive. They hung around a lot at Elizabethan fayres."

"I'd like being a rascally rabble and riff-raff, Dad. You know, nicking stuff. When can we start?"

"Er," says Dad, catching Mum's eye, "on second thoughts, perhaps that's not a very good idea. We'll think of something else." Dad leaps up out of his chair. "Time to do some research, kids. Let's get into that Elizabethan mood!"

"To the library, Dad?" says Rupert, dragging on Dad's sleeve.

"You bet. Let's dig for some details."

That's another Rent-a-Rabble slogan: *The*

Drama's in the Detail. "The ordinary details of ordinary lives," raves Dad. "Now, that's really exciting!"

"Really exciting, Dad!" repeats Rupert, like a parrot.

"For instance," Dad says, "here's a detail to conjure with. Did you know that when Elizabethans wore extra-big ruffs, they had to have extra-long spoons to eat with?"

"Wow!" says Rupert as if it's the most fascinating fact he's ever heard. "That's not the kind of thing you ever think about, is it, Dad?"

My big brother, Ryan, drifts in. It seems that, as usual, he's not listening. He's in a world of his own, thinking about gadgets and inventions. But then he says, "Ruff spoons? Dad, I could invent you a really great ruff spoon. A new, modern, improved version."

"But it wouldn't be authentic then, would it, Ryan?" Dad points out, patiently.

I don't know why he bothers. He's had this argument with Ryan a thousand times. But Ryan can't help improving on history. All their lo-tech gadgets give him itchy fingers.

He's just got to improve them and bring them right up to date.

"I've told you before," Dad reminds him. "It's not our job to improve on history. 'Rent-a-Rabble Tells It Like It Was'."

Just as I thought, Ryan takes no notice. He's already scribbling notes and plans on his hand.

"Let's get going, Dad!" shouts Rupert, as if Dad has promised to take him for a day out at Quasar Quest.

I sigh. Sometimes it feels like I'm living with a load of lunatics. I'm not counting Mum of course. Mum's an accountant. She's quite normal.

Rebel, our historical hound, is the other sane member of the family. You haven't met him yet. He's gone roaming somewhere. Rebel's his own dog. He won't beg or fetch sticks for humans. He's got too much self-respect. Sometimes, I think he's wiser than any human I know.

Rupert and Dad go rushing out to our old, blue Rent-a-Rabble van. Dad stuck a new poster on it yesterday. He said, "This one's really snappy!"

It says:

Need a peasant, a churl,
or an underling?
Then pick up that phone and
give us a ring!

When we drive by, you can see people scratching their heads. They're probably saying, "Doh! What's that all about?" I think Dad's got a lot to learn about advertising.

Mum gives me a questioning look. She says, "Aren't you going with them, Rae?"

I've got my own plans for Saturday morning and they don't include going to the library. In fact, I've been seriously thinking about backing out of Rent-a-Rabble altogether. Dad paid us a measly five pounds for that medieval job. Even though me and Ryan worked our butts off!

But then Mum says, like she's making a confession, "I wish I could give Dad more help with Rent-a-Rabble. I'm just too busy at work. So it's a real comfort to me that Dad's got you to rely on."

I'm left thinking, *That's not fair, that's*

blackmail! And, *You can't load this on to me.* And, *Why should I do it for five quid?* But I'm too soft-hearted for my own good.

"OK, Mum, I'm going."

I give a big sigh to show I'm doing her a big, big favour. Then I get up off my chair and trudge after Dad and Rupert.

I stop at the door, "You coming, Ryan?"

Ryan looks at me in that dozy way he's got, as if to say, "Who are you, exactly?" Don't be fooled though. My brother might look a bit slow from the outside. But inside his head his thoughts are whizzing round like the whirligigs on our pond.

"Errr," he finally answers, "no, I'm busy. I got things to make. I'll catch you later." And he wanders out of the kitchen.

I know what he's going to do. He's going to try to improve on history. Dad isn't going to like that one little bit.

Chapter Two

I'm sitting on a blue bean bag in the library flicking through a book about Queen Elizabeth. I don't know who I'll be yet at the Elizabethan Fayre. But I'm glad it's not going to be her. She wore a bright red wig and had chalky white make-up and black teeth. And she only took a bath about once a year. I suppose none of her best friends told her. For starters, because they all smelled the same. And for seconds, because they didn't want their heads chopped off.

There's something tickling my ear.

I put my right hand up to scratch it.

"Yay!" yells Rupert. "It works!"

He waggles a bit of straw at me.

"Rupert, stop playing stupid games!"

"I'm not playing stupid games. I'm doing serious research."

"What you talking about?"

"Elizabethan people wore purses tied to their belts. Right? And they walked round with their hands on their purses. Right? So no one could nick them."

"Get to the point!"

"So these sneaky thieves called cutpurses, they tickled your ear with a piece of straw. And when you scratched yourself, they cut off your purse with a sharp dagger. Dad, Dad, can I have a sharp dagger?" Rupert's voice goes booming across the library. "So I can nick people's purses?"

"Shhh! Shhh!" I tell him. People are looking shocked. Ladies are nervously clutching their handbags.

"Anyway, where did you get that straw?"

"It was stuck in my jumper. It's from my hamster cage. I was cleaning him out before breakfast."

"Ughh! Don't tickle my ear with that. That's revolting."

It's no good telling Rupert that. He loves anything revolting. For our last job he made himself an expert on the Middle Ages. And he's thrilled to bits that some things haven't changed. Especially for peasants.

"They're still wiping their bums on big leaves!" he tells me, in a foghorn voice that echoes round the bookshelves.

"You don't have to shout. Why do you always have to shout?"

I think he does it on purpose. He loves being the centre of attention.

"And there were some terrible tortures. There was this one where they heated up these pincers until they were red hot—"

"Rupert!" Dad comes bounding over. It's the end of his nice, peaceful read. "Time for a Coke in the café," he says, through gritted teeth. I think sometimes he wishes Rupert wouldn't get quite so enthusiastic.

"Dad! Dad!" Rupert drags on Dad's arm. "I want to get this book out. Guess what? It's about a guy who invented this posh flushing toilet for Queen Elizabeth. Nobody in those days had seen anything like it! They were still emptying potties out their windows and shouting, 'Gardez Loo!'"

Oh no. Rupert's found two things that fascinate him about Elizabethan times – toilets and torture. And, if we don't stop him, he's going to go on and on and on about them.

"Let's get him out of here," I hiss at Dad. Dad doesn't need telling twice.

The library café is crowded with people taking a break from reading books.

One man we pass puts his hand to his ear. He brushes away at it, like a dog having a scratch.

"Works every time!" whispers Rupert, sticking his straw back into his jumper.

"Will you stop doing that!"

"And another thing I found out," Rupert says eagerly, as soon as we sit down. "When they cut traitors' heads off they stuck them on poles until they rotted. Isn't that interesting?"

A woman next to us puts down her doughnut. Oh, no, it's happening again. On our medieval job, Rupert emptied a café when he talked about the symptoms of the Black Death.

Dad remembers that too. He's just come back with some crisps and Coke and yoghurts on a tray. He's frantic to change the subject.

"This book I've got on Elizabethan fayres is really fascinating, Rupert." Dad takes the battered old book out of his pocket and opens it. "You know I was talking about those poor, unfortunate folk displayed as freaks—?"

"No, I'm not being a Bearded Lady," I interrupt to remind him.

"Well, this guy wasn't a freak exactly. I suppose he was more of an entertainer really, like the jugglers and acrobats."

Rupert actually shuts up and listens. He pops his crisp packet open with a loud *bang!* and starts to chomp them.

"*He can make his face as small as an apple,*" reads Dad. "*He turns his mouth into the shape of a bird's beak, makes his eyes like an owl, lolls his tongue out a foot long and licks his nose like a cow. Makes one eyebrow go up and the other down. Then changes his face so as to appear like a grisly corpse long buried.*"

The woman at the next table puts her doughnut down again.

"Wow!" shouts Rupert, spitting out crisp crumbs. You can see he's impressed. "Could I be that face-maker, Dad, at our Elizabethan Fayre? It'd be really authentic, wouldn't it? I'll practise, honest. Look, I can already do the eyebrows."

And he's just jiggling his eyebrows about like two dancing furry caterpillars when Ryan walks into the café. He dodges through the crowded tables. Then dumps his backpack in front of Dad.

"I've made them," he tells him.

"Made what?" asks Dad, looking warily at the backpack.

"Those ruff spoons you were talking about."

"Oh, those!" says Dad, relaxing. I know what he's thinking. He's thinking, "Spoons are harmless enough. Even Ryan can't modernize spoons much." Because you never know with Ryan's new, improved versions of things. They can give you a nasty shock – if you're not prepared.

"OK," says Ryan. "Let's try them out. Let's do a little experiment. I didn't have time to make proper ruffs. So you'll just have to improvise."

He grabs the whole pile of white serviettes from the counter. The lady serving tea and coffee gives him a glare. She must think we're really messy eaters.

"Oh, I see!" says Dad, taking a fistful of serviettes.

I can't believe it. He's going along with it! He's taking Ryan's experiment seriously. He's actually tucking the serviettes into his neck so they look like a big frilly collar. So is Rupert. He always copies Dad.

"Look, Dad, I've got a ruff too."

"Yes, Rupert. That's very attractive."

Can't they see people nudging each other and whispering? "People are looking," I hiss.

That doesn't bother Ryan. He never notices other people much. Like I said before, he's on his own planet most of the time. It doesn't bother Dad either. When he's thinking about history the modern world doesn't exist. And Rupert likes showing off, anyway. Am I the only one here who ever gets embarrassed? Mum wouldn't show herself up like this. But she isn't here to back me up. I'm outnumbered by loonies.

So I just tuck some serviettes round the neck of my T-shirt. "Get this over with quickly! All right?" I warn Ryan in my most dangerous voice. Maybe only a few people will notice.

"Your ruff doesn't stick out enough, Rae," says Dad, looking critically at my serviettes. "Real ruffs were stiff with starch." He gives my serviettes a tweak. "That's better."

"For heaven's sake. I look like a clown's dog now!" I sneak a look round the café. Thank goodness no one I know is here.

"Did you know," says Dad, "that hundreds of poor washerwomen in London made a meagre living from laundering ruffs?"

My dad amazes me. Doesn't he know it's not normal to wear pretend ruffs in public? He's not self-conscious at all. He's sitting there chatting away, as if it's something

17

everyone does all the time. That's what being a history nut does for you.

"Some ruffs were huge," Dad informs us. "They were called cartwheel ruffs. Those were the ones you needed really long spoons for."

"I've thought of that," says Ryan, opening his back-pack. "Doesn't matter how big your ruff is. It could be a metre wide! You can still reach your mouth. Because my special spoons are extendable."

Doubt comes creeping back into Dad's voice. "But I can't remember reading about extendable ruff spoons," he protests. "I don't think they had them in Elizabethan times."

"They didn't," agrees Ryan. "But they should have done. I've invented them now, anyway. So at least you lot can use them."

It's useless for Dad to go on about it not being authentic. Ryan's really enthusiastic about his invention. He can't see why Dad's raising so many objections.

Ryan shares out his new improved ruff spoons.

"Hey!" says Rupert, inspecting his spoon. "This is brilliant! It's like that grabber thing

Gran picks things off the floor with. Only with a spoon on the end."

"That's what gave me the idea," says Ryan. "Now, you just load up your spoon. Point it at your mouth. Squeeze the end of the handle gently and, hey presto, the handle extends."

"All right," Dad gives in. "We'll give them a try."

We each scoop a spoonful of chocolate yoghurt. Then raise our ruff spoons.

"Now, squeeze those spoons," instructs Ryan.

It works! My handle shoots out.

But it misses my mouth altogether. It boings past my ear. How long is this spoon? Help, I can't control it! The handle's got a life of its own. It won't stop extending. It's whipping about in my hand like a bendy branch. It's swaying around in the air like a spoon-headed snake!

Whoops. A dollop of brown stuff flies out of my spoon. It shoots over people's heads. *Splat!* It makes a messy splodge on the opposite wall and slowly trickles down.

The others aren't so lucky.

"Argh!" yells Dad as his spoon extends and misses his mouth too. It bonks him on the nose. "Ow!" Then flicks round and dumps yoghurt into his ear. The handle escapes from his hand. It flies for his neck and loops itself round like an octopus tentacle.

"It's attacking me!"

Dad's having a fight with his extendable spoon, trying to wrench it from round his throat.

"Hey!"

"Look out!"

Two cries of distress from somewhere in the café tell me what's happened to Ryan's and Rupert's yoghurt. It's gone catapulting through the air and bombed some poor people. Quite a lot of people really. Everyone seems to be wiping it off their clothes, out of their hair. It's all over the place. How can two spoonfuls of yoghurt splatter so far?

"Where's your ruff spoon?" I shout at Ryan.

"Er, I couldn't hold on to it. It's escaped. It's over there somewhere."

Oh, no! It's writhing on the floor between

tables. There's a woman trying to stamp it to death.

"Oh, dear," says Ryan, calmly. "I think they're a bit uncontrollable, aren't they? I made the handles too long. And too springy." He scribbles a few modifications on his hand.

"Just a few minor problems," he mutters to himself. The café's in chaos all around him. But he doesn't seem to notice. He's already back in a world of his own. "I'll get it right next time," he tells Dad.

"There isn't going to be a next time!" gasps Dad. He's panting hard. His face is all red. He looks quite upset. There are broken bits of ruff spoon in his hand. "This thing went wild! It tried to strangle me. It wrapped itself twice round my neck!"

Dad pulls a few of the serviettes out his neck and uses them to wipe his face. He looks round for the first time. People in the café are making angry remarks. One woman's saying, "What about my dry-cleaning bill?" Someone else says, "I've just had my hair blow-dried!"

Dad shakes himself back into the twenty-first century. Even he seems to realize we're

21

in deep trouble. I'm cringing inside. I wish the ground would open and swallow me up. Maybe if I pretend I'm not a Rabble, that I've never seen them before in my life. That they're aliens from the planet Zarg. . .

But it's too late. Some people are getting up out of their seats, heading towards our table. It looks like it could get nasty.

Rupert's trying to scrunch his ruff spoon up small. But it doesn't want to go back. The handle's flopping and twisting about all over the place, like a toddler having a tantrum.

"Just leave that alone!" I warn him. "Put it down. That thing's dangerous!"

But Rupert thinks it's great. "Hey, this is really good fun! I want to shoot it out again. How do you make it go back?"

"Oh, dear," says Ryan vaguely. "I never thought about that."

"Come on, kids," says Dad, dragging Rupert by the scruff of the neck and heading for the way out. "It's time to make a move."

Chapter Three

We have to call in at the supermarket on the way home. Mum gave us a list. Dad forgot all about it until I reminded him.

In the van we take off our Elizabethan ruffs. We look nearly normal again. Except there are yoghurt smears all over Dad's jumper from the Attack of the Killer Spoons.

When we get to the supermarket Ryan says he'll wait in the van. He says he's got a lot of thinking to do.

I hope he's not thinking about making more ruff spoons. I don't want to see another ruff spoon for the rest of my life. It wasn't one of Ryan's best inventions. Not like that stealth armour he made for the medieval job. Now that was sheer genius.

Dad's looking round the shelves in a puzzled way. "What are we in here for?"

I consult Mum's list. It's neatly typed. She did it on her laptop computer.

"Ham and mushroom pizza," I tell Dad. "And milk and –"

Rupert's looking bored. No one's paid any attention to him for at least five minutes. So he grabs a potato.

"Zounds!" he cries out in a really loud voice. "By my troth! What is this strange, knobbly, brown thing. Do you eat it or smoke it?"

"Stop showing off!" I tell Rupert. "Everyone knows about Sir Walter Raleigh. Even I know he brought tobacco and potatoes back from America."

"But did you know," says Rupert, "that when Sir Walter smoked his pipe his servant thought he was on fire and chucked a pot of ale over him?"

I didn't know that. But I'm not about to admit it. It'll make Rupert even more big-headed. But then Dad says, "Excellent historical detail, son! I can see you're really getting into the Elizabethan mood."

Rupert looks smug. When will Dad learn that encouraging him only makes him a million times worse?

Dad drifts off down the aisles. A man wanders past, inspecting the cans of soup. Suddenly he lifts his hand. He scratches behind his ear like an itchy dog.

Rupert looks amazed. "Did you see that, Rae? It worked again. It always works!"

"Give me that straw!"

"No, Rae, I'm practising being a cutpurse."

"There's no way Dad's going to let you be a cutpurse at the Fayre. Not if it involves sharp daggers and nicking money. Dream on!"

Rupert starts sulking. His bottom lip sticks out like a fat, pink slug.

"Anyway, I thought you were going to be an

entertainer, like that guy who made faces?"

"Hey! I forgot about that!" says Rupert, instantly cheering up.

A woman is passing with a baby buggy. She turns her back to take something from the top shelves. Rupert sticks his head into the buggy.

There's a terrified howl: "Waaaa!"

Rupert skips away looking innocent. The woman shoots him a suspicious glare and hurries off.

But I know what he's been doing. Dad appears at the end of the aisle. "Dad, Dad, Rupert's been scaring babies!"

"Oh, dear," says Dad vaguely. "Don't do that, Rupert. Their mums might not like it."

Sometimes I could give Dad a good shake. Why does he let Rupert get away with things? I wasn't allowed to, when I was his age.

Rupert's twisting his face into ghastly shapes. "I can make my mouth into a bird's beak. And do owl eyes. And make my eyebrows go up and down. That's easy peasy. But I can't lick my nose with my tongue yet. See?"

"Yuck, put your tongue away! It's disgusting! It's all yellow and furry. No wonder that little kid screamed."

"I was just entertaining it. With my funny faces." Rupert rolls up his eyes until only the whites show, and sucks in his cheeks so hard his head looks like a skull. "Is this how you make your face look like a grisly corpse long buried?"

Dad comes back with some more shopping. He looks alarmed. "What on earth's wrong with Rupert?"

"He's just pretending to be a corpse long buried."

"Perhaps you should do that in private, son."

As usual, Rupert takes notice. For about ten seconds. There are long queues at the checkouts. While Dad and me wait he manages to slip away.

"Where's Rupert gone now?" asks Dad, looking anxiously round.

"Waaaa!" There's an ear-splitting scream like a jet breaking the sound barrier. Then another: "Waaaa!" Then another. I have to put my hands over my ears. It's enough to give you a headache. Mums and dads are looking harassed. They're getting really stressed out. Every baby in the queue is going bananas!

Me and Dad look at each other.

"Rupert!" Dad hisses. "I'll kill him!"

That's more like it. It's about time Dad got more strict.

"What's wrong with the kids in this supermarket?" complains Rupert, as Dad frogmarches him outside. "I was only trying to entertain them while they waited. They've just got no sense of humour."

There's a hairdresser's next to the supermarket. Dad trudges ahead with the shopping. Rupert darts over to the hairdresser's window before I can stop him. "Look who's in there," he says.

It's that wily little weasel, and our arch enemy, Nigel – with Raymond, his best friend and minder.

They're waiting to get their hair cut. At least Nigel is. Raymond can't be because his head is shaved already. He's scowling. He looks like a giant pickled onion in a very bad mood.

I turn away quickly from the window. I hope he didn't see me spying. I don't want to get mixed up with them. We had a lot of trouble with them at our medieval job. They probably still want revenge. Don't ask me to explain. I'd rather forget all about it.

But Rupert goes skipping inside! How reckless is that? I just don't understand him. He doesn't seem to recognize danger. He seems to think he's got a guardian angel to get him out of any sticky situation. I suppose he has in a way. It's me.

I give a deep sigh and follow him inside.

Soon as I'm in there, I know Rupert's stepped right into trouble. Raymond's already looking puzzled. Something Rupert said must have made him think. That's a dangerous thing to do, make Raymond think. Usually Nigel does his thinking for him.

"I told you, you shouldn't be sitting waiting like that," says Rupert. "You should be playing the lute."

Raymond's bald head scrunches up like a naked mole rat. He doesn't understand. And that makes him get upset.

"Do I hear a stinking Rabble speaking, Raymond?" says Nigel looking round as if Rupert is invisible. That's Nigel's idea of humour.

"Did you know that in Elizabethan times," shouts Rupert in his boomy voice, "people were mad about tunes and singing and that? And barber's shops had lutes in them? So people waiting for a haircut could pluck a lute and sing madrigals?"

"Madrigals?" says Raymond, frowning. "What you on about?"

Rupert stops for a think. He's wondering how to explain madrigals to Raymond. He gives up and just sings one. "Hey nonny nonny no, hey nonny, nonny no, hey nonny, nonny no. That's a madrigal."

Why is he singing through his nose like that? In that horrible shrill voice that sounds like fingernails down a blackboard? "Will you shut up?" I hiss at him. "Let's get going!"

Too late.

"I think you're trying to be cheeky, Rabble," says Nigel, with a smirky smile.

"This is another one," announces Rupert. "Hey ring a ding a ding. Hey ring a ding a ding. You and Raymond could sing that. Hey ring a ding a ding a ding a –"

He's going on and on and on in that high screechy whine. He can't seem to stop himself. "Hey ring a ding a ding." It's doing my head in. Even I want to swat him, like a wasp.

I twist his ear, as if I'm turning off a radio. That should do the trick. It doesn't.

"Hey ring a – gerroff, Rae! – ding a ding, hey ring a –"

"He's getting on my nerves, Raymond," says Nigel. "It's time he got taught a lesson."

Like a big, bad-tempered grizzly bear, Raymond lurches out of his chair.

"Wait! He's just a little kid," I plead with Nigel. "He's loony actually. Completely round the bend. You only have to listen to him."

"Hey nonny, nonny, nonny, no –"

Raymond pauses for a second. He looks at Nigel for further instructions.

I try desperately to take their minds off Rupert. I say the first thing that comes into my head. "You going to the Elizabethan Fayre on Saturday?" I ask Raymond.

31

Nigel answers for him. "What, that boring Fayre? Nah, we wouldn't be seen dead at that."

I breathe a sigh of relief. At least that's one thing I don't have to worry about.

"But my mum's going to be there," says Nigel. "She's in charge of everything. So you Rabbles had better behave yourselves."

"Hey ring a ding a ding." Is Rupert still singing madrigals? He's going a strange purple colour.

"Are you all right? Take a breath!" I whack him hard on the back. He chokes, then sucks in a great lungful of air. At least he's stopped ring-a-ding-dinging. Phew, thank goodness. How did the Elizabethans stand it? I couldn't stand it for five minutes.

"Come on," I drag Rupert away.

We have to pass close to Raymond to get out of the shop. He reaches up and bats like mad at his right ear. "Eh? Wossat?"

Outside I give Rupert a good shake.

"Just what do you think you're doing? Hey-nonny-noing and poking that straw into Raymond's ear? Have you got a deathwish or something?"

"But it's true, that is," Rupert protests. "About lutes in barber's shops. And about madrigals. Like hey ring a ding a—"

"Don't you dare start all that again!" I threaten him. "Stop it RIGHT NOW! It's really, really irritating. It makes me want to scream!""

He can see I'm really mad this time. "We only just got out of there alive!" I tell him.

After I've calmed down a bit, I ask him, "Rupert, why do you deliberately try to get on people's nerves?"

He looks at me, all wide-eyed and innocent. As if he doesn't have a clue what I'm talking about. "It's not fair," he starts whining. "It's not my fault. I just open my mouth. And people get mad! Don't ask me why."

It's been a tough day. You've probably noticed, in the Rabble family, history is a really tiring business. So when we get out to the van, it's great to see Rebel, our streetwise historical hound.

"Hey, Rebel, you're back!"

Don't ask me where he's been. Or how he knew where we were. He always tracks us down. He's outside the van with Ryan.

Ryan's giving him lots of welcome-home pats.

Everyone's pleased to see Rebel. But I'm thrilled to bits. Just when you think you're the only sane person, when it seems like the whole world's going nuts, Rebel turns up.

He doesn't fawn round me. He's too cool for that. He just raises his bushy eyebrows, as if to say, "Have these history-freaks been giving you a hard time?" We understand each other, me and Rebel.

Driving back home, Dad says, "We've got to make some decisions, kids. The Elizabethan Fayre is next Saturday. We've done our research. So we've got to decide what we're going to be."

"What about you being Sir Walter Raleigh?" suggests Rupert. "He had this beard that curled up at the end. It drove ladies wild!"

"Did it ?" says Dad. "That's an interesting detail." Then he gives himself a good shake. Rent-a-Rabble isn't supposed to be interested in the rich and famous.

"No, I'm afraid I can't be him, Rupert. Rent-a-Rabble never plays nobles. We only play peasants and humble folk who had to crook their knees all the time."

"How do you crook your knee, Dad?" asks Rupert.

"You bow, you idiot," I tell him. "Dad means poor, humble people who had to go round grovelling to nobles."

"I could be a coachman, Dad," says Rupert. "Some rich people used them as footstools to climb in and out of their coaches. Is a human footstool humble enough?"

"A human footstool is certainly humble," muses Dad. "That's right up Rent-a-Rabble's street. But I'm afraid there won't be any coaches there on Saturday."

"Then what about a rat catcher, Dad? They went round Elizabethan fayres. Then Rebel could be a rat catcher's dog."

I glance at Rebel. He doesn't seem to object. "You'd be good as a rat catcher's dog," I tell him.

"That's not a bad idea, Rupert," agrees Dad. "Course you'd have to have lots of dead rats dangling from your belt."

"Excellent!" says Rupert.

"And hold up a big sign with a rat on it."

"I could do that. I'm class at drawing rats."

"Why do you need a sign?" I can't help asking.

"Because hardly anyone could read," says Rupert. "And when they saw the sign they'd say, 'There's goes a rat catcher.' Say if you were a Bearded Lady—"

"Which I'm not going to be!" I remind him. That's one thing I definitely won't change my mind about.

"No, but if you were, you'd have to hold up a big sign with a big, bushy beard on it. And people would say, 'Hey, there goes a Bearded Lady!'"

There's something wrong with that. "That's stupid!" I tell Rupert. But, somehow, I can't explain why.

"No, it isn't," he argues.

"Yes, it is."

Then Ryan's voice comes from behind a box of props. I forgot he was in the van with us. Ryan's like that. Sometimes he's so lost in his own thoughts that he doesn't speak for hours.

"This book's really ace," he says. "It's giving me lots of great ideas."

"What book?"

"This book about Sir John Harrington that Rupert got out of the library. He was Queen Elizabeth's godson. It says he invented a flushing toilet in 1592."

"How interesting," I reply.

"I know, it is, isn't it?" says Rupert.

"I was being sarcastic!"

I don't know why I bother. Rupert's getting like Dad. If you try to be sarcastic about history, Dad always takes you seriously.

"That Sir John was interested in toilets, just like I am," Rupert carries on eagerly. "And he knew loads of rude jokes. Did you know he got banned from Court for telling rude jokes? He's my hero, actually," adds Rupert, with a star-struck look in his eyes.

"There's even a drawing of his invention in here," says Ryan, as if he's made a thrilling discovery.

"Really?" says Dad. Oh, no, I don't believe it, he's getting all excited too. "Is it an authentic drawing? With all the details from Elizabethan times?"

"Yep. And it's dead simple. The Queen's Privy, it's called. I could make this privy, Dad, no problem!"

Here we go. I'm outnumbered again. Everyone but me is talking about Elizabethan toilets. And everyone seems to find them fascinating.

"I could make quite a few improvements," adds Ryan, studying the drawing. But I don't think Dad heard him say that.

I glance at Rebel. He raises his eyebrows. I raise mine back. It's a bit pathetic really. The person who understands me best, in the whole of our family, just happens to be a dog.

Chapter Four

It's tea time. We're sitting at the table when Mum asks a question. I don't know what it is about my mum. But she's the opposite of Dad. Sort of brisk and efficient, where Dad's waffly. Mum concentrates your mind.

"So what are you going to be at the Elizabethan Fayre on Saturday?" she asks us.

I'm surprised she's interested. Mum

doesn't take any part in Rent-a-Rabble, except to keep the accounts. She thinks it's a GOOD THING though, because it keeps Dad busy. After he lost his job at the History Museum Dad got really depressed.

We all look a bit guilty. Except for Ryan of course. He's not paying attention, even to Mum. He's scribbling away on a piece of paper. Is it ruff spoons or the Queen's personal privy? Don't ask me. Ryan's mind is a mystery to anyone normal.

"Err," confesses Dad. "We haven't actually made up our minds yet."

"Have you got to make your own costumes?" asks Mum.

"That won't take long," I tell her.

It never takes long with Rent-a-Rabble. Just a few old rags and we're ready.

"The reason I'm asking," says Mum, "is that I'm going to be there on Saturday."

"What, really?" says Dad, pleased and surprised.

Mum hasn't been at any of our jobs so far. Good thing, really. They've all been a bit disastrous. It wasn't all Rent-a-Rabble's fault. We've just had a lot of bad luck.

"Yes," says Mum, "I'm coming to the Elizabethan Fayre with some important Japanese clients. They want to see a slice of really authentic British history. We'll be in the VIP tent and on the platform at the prizegiving. I hear it's going to be quite jolly – stalls selling gingerbread and ale. Jugglers and minstrels and dancing bears. My clients are looking forward to it."

I'm thinking, *That sounds OK. At least we'll be in the fresh air this time, not stuck in some dark, smoky hovel*, when Rupert shouts, "Dancing bears? No way! That's cruel!"

Dad says soothingly, "Don't get upset, Rupert. They're not real dancing bears. They're people in costumes."

Then Rupert says, "I bet they don't look like real bears."

"But you don't want them to be real bears!" Honestly, if there was an exam in being awkward my little brother would come top.

"They had dancing dogs at fayres as well," says Dad. "Hang on a sec, that gives me an idea. You don't think Rebel –?"

"Don't even think about it, Dad," I warn him.

Rebel, the coolest dog in the world, dancing for humans? Dream on!

"Dancing dogs is cruel as well!" says Rupert who can't stand being quiet for a second.

"Oh, shut up, Rupert! Everyone knows that."

"Hey nonny nonny no, hey nonny, nonny nonny, nonny, nonny!" Rupert goes on and on and on as if someone's wound him up.

I cram my hands over my ears. "Dad, make him stop. It's torture!"

"Kids! Kids!" says Dad, banging on the table to restore order. "Mum's going to be there on Saturday. So Rent-a-Rabble must make an extra effort. We mustn't fight amongst ourselves. We're a team, remember. A slick and professional team."

If Rebel was here we'd both raise our eyebrows at that bit. But he isn't here. He's out in the street, sniffing things.

"Right, sir, Captain sir," says Rupert, giving Dad a salute. I told you he's a little creep.

Behind Dad's back, he sticks his tongue out at me as far as he can.

"Hey, Dad, did you see what Rupert just did?"

"I'm just practising," he tells Dad, trying hard to lick his nose. "These are authentic Elizabethan funny faces."

But I haven't got time to quarrel with Rupert. I've got a question to ask. Something Mum just said made me curious. "Mum, what do you mean you're going to be at the prizegiving? What prizegiving?"

"Didn't you know? The Lady Mayoress is going to present fifty pounds to the winner of the best Elizabethan costume at the Fayre."

Fifty pounds! Rent-a-Rabble could do with that cash. But then I immediately think, *We've got no chance!* Other people will be wearing gorgeous costumes. Big ruffs, and silk and velvet clothes stiff with jewels and embroidery. While we'll be wearing rags. Or scratchy brown coal sacks, if we're lucky. That's not going to win us any prizes, is it? Even if it is authentic.

I'm just thinking, *Forget about the*

competition, Rae, when Rupert shouts across the table.

"Dad! Dad! I've decided what I want to be! I'm not going to be a rat catcher."

Dad looks amazed that someone has actually made a decision. "Really?"

"I'm going to be someone ever so downtrodden and probably a bit pongy as well. I'm going to be The Keeper of the Queen's Privy."

"What, an Elizabethan toilet attendant?" I can't help sneering. "You just made that up. Get real!"

"Is that authentic?" Dad asks, doubtfully.

"Well, Queen Elizabeth wouldn't clean her toilet herself, would she?" says Rupert.

"Rupert's right," says Dad, getting all excited. "There must have been someone to clean it. The Keeper of the Queen's Privy, or whatever his official title was, has been entirely neglected by history. He's just the kind of completely forgotten person that Rent-a-Rabble loves!"

"And better than that!" shouts Rupert, encouraged by Dad's enthusiasm. "Ryan is going to build me a full-size model of Queen Elizabeth's loo. Aren't you, Ryan?"

Rupert pokes Ryan in the ribs. Ryan looks up vaguely and says, "What?"

Warning bells are clanging like mad in my brain. "Dad? Do you think that's a good idea?"

Mum's going to be there on Saturday. We want her to be proud of us. When Ryan makes things you never know what's going to happen. "Remember the ruff spoons?" I ask Dad.

There's another thing. "Have you told Rebel?" I ask Rupert. "He was going to be a rat catcher's dog. What's he going to be now? A privy keeper's dog? He's not going to like that."

But no one's listening to me. Rupert's saying, "We've got to take a privy to the Fayre. How can I be Keeper of the Queen's Privy if her privy isn't there?"

I bet Dad's got doubts, just like I have. But he hates discouraging kids. He thinks it might traumatize them or something. So he just says, "Right ho! Let's get to work!"

If I ever have kids I'm not going to be like Dad. I'm going to be really strict with them.

Mum might have backed me up. But Rent-a-Rabble is Dad's business. And she doesn't want to interfere. So she just asks Dad, "Richard, what are you going to be at the Fayre?"

"I'm going to be one of the rabblement of course," says Dad. "Those wretched creatures who were forced by land enclosures to roam the countryside and beg and steal to survive."

"That's not very nice," objects Mum. "Are you sure that's what people want to see?"

"It's what they need to see!" Dad insists sternly. "Rent-a-Rabble isn't here to make history nice. We tell it like it was! Warts and all!"

"Hang on," Mum suggests quickly, before Dad gets really carried away. "What about that lovely Elizabethan costume up in the loft? Remember, you made it to put on display at the History Museum years ago? It would be a pity to waste it."

Dad looks horrified, as if Mum's asked him to commit a terrible crime. "But I can't wear that costume! I'd feel like a traitor to Rent-a-Rabble. That's a nobleman's costume. It's got a jewelled doublet and cloak, a big ruff, crimson padded breeches, stockings with fancy garters. And even gold lace wrist ruffles. Things no poor person would ever be able to afford."

"Wow! Crimson breeches! Fancy garters! Wrist ruffles! It sounds class, Dad!" I've just had a brilliant brainwave. "Dad, if you wear that, you could win the prize for best costume, easy-peasy. It's fifty pounds. Rent-a-Rabble could really do with that money."

"No, Rae!" says Dad. He looks stubborn. "Don't try to persuade me. It's a question of principle. I shall never, ever wear that costume. Not even if the prize was a million pounds!"

Chapter Five

There are only two days now to the Elizabethan Fayre. I still haven't decided what I'm going to be. Strange things are happening in our house. For a start, Ryan's locked himself in the garage. I can hear lots of hammering. But he won't let anyone see what he's doing.

Rupert's hanging around outside when I get

home. "He's making a model of the queen's privy," he says proudly. "So I can be Keeper of it. Did you know that at Greenwich Palace they had a privy that twenty-eight people could use at once? How efficient is that?"

"Yes, very interesting," I tell him. "But are you sure Ryan's making you the authentic flush toilet? You know, the 1592 version, just like the picture in the history book? He didn't say anything about modernizing it, did he?"

"No," said Rupert. "He wouldn't do that."

Want to bet?

The other strange thing is the way Dad's behaving.

I caught him last night taking a sneaky look in my wardrobe mirror. He had the Elizabethan costume on. The one from up in the loft. He looked more gorgeous than a peacock. He had sparkly jewels all over his doublet. And a velvet hat with purple plumes and crimson padded breeches and white stockings and high-heeled shoes with silver buckles. And, I forgot, a huge ruff round his neck.

I said, "I thought you weren't going to wear all that posh gear at the Fayre."

He spun round, looking really guilty. He said, "Oh, Rae, I didn't know you were there. I'm just trying it out. You didn't think I was actually going to wear it, did you? No, Rent-a-Rabble will be wearing scratchy peasant-style tunics, dyed with conker skins."

"You mean brown. That's sooo dreary! Why do we always have to wear brown stuff? Wear that, Dad! Go on! It's brilliant. You look like a rainbow. You'll win the costume competition for sure. Who are you supposed to be?"

"Well, technically, I'm an Elizabethan gallant, I suppose," said Dad, admiring himself in the mirror. "You know, a rich, fashionable young lord about town. Popular and handsome. Complimenting ladies at Court and making witty conversation –"

Dad suddenly stopped. The dreamy look went out of his eyes. He gave himself a good shake, as if he was making himself come to his senses. "But of course I couldn't possibly wear it. That's out of the question!"

I thought, *Well, at least you tried, Rae.*

I didn't have much hope. Dad's really

strict about the principles of Rent-a-Rabble. *Serfs 'R' Us!* it says on our van. How can you be a lord with a slogan like that?

But when I go into the house I'm amazed to see Dad dressed up again as an Elizabethan gallant.

Before I can say anything, he starts explaining. "Rae, I've been thinking about what you said last night. And I've decided to make a big sacrifice. For the sake of the business, I'm going to force myself to be a lord just for one day. I'm going to enter that costume competition."

"Brilliant, Dad! You'll win it easy!"

Is it my imagination, or has he been altering his costume? That ruff seems much bigger than yesterday. It's so big he can hardly get through the door!

"Dad, go out and show Ryan. He's making a privy in the garage."

"I can't do that," says Dad fussily, polishing a jewel on his doublet. "It's raining. My ruff will go all floppy."

Since when has Dad worried about rain ruining his clothes? He never cared about fashion. He's the scruffiest dad in the world, the universe. He wears baggy old jumpers full of holes.

But now he's inspecting his stockings in the mirror. "Do my calves look big in these?" he asks me.

"No," I tell him. He looks dead disappointed. I think I gave the wrong answer. But Dad's always had spindly chicken legs. They look even more skinny in those white tights. Especially when he's wearing padded breeches shaped like an enormous pumpkin.

"But an Elizabethan gallant had to show a fine leg," he says.

"Eh?"

"Ladies in those days admired fine, manly, swelling calves."

"I don't think you've got calves, Dad. You must have been born without them."

I can't see a swelling at all, even the size of a pimple, between Dad's knee and his ankle.

"I'll have to pad my tights," Dad decides.

I laugh. "Come on, Dad, you're kidding me."

"No, that's what they really did," he

protests. "They stuffed their calves with bran to make their legs look big! If I've got to give up my principles and be a lord, I might as well make him authentic."

"Bran's no good," says a voice in the doorway.

It's Ryan. He's finally come out of the garage. He must have finished Queen Elizabeth's privy.

"Bran's too prickly," he tells Dad. "And what happens when it gets wet? It'll swell and split your tights."

"Good point, son," says Dad.

Ryan starts scribbling away on his hand. "I could make you a calf-expander, Dad. No worries!"

"Dad!" I hiss at him urgently. "Remember the ruff spoons."

But Dad hardly seems to be listening. He's looking at himself in the mirror again.

He sticks one leg and one arm out. He tries a low, sweeping bow. But he can't bend in the middle in all those padded clothes.

"I' faith my lady," he says. "Your lips are like cherries, your skin is like milk."

"And your teeth are like stars, 'cos they

come out at night," adds Rupert, suddenly appearing in the doorway.

We laugh. "I don't think you kids are taking this seriously," complains Dad, in a wounded voice. "I'm only trying to get the feel of the character."

"What character?" asks Rupert.

"The one I'm going to be at the Fayre, of course. Sir Walter Rabble, dashing young lord and Queen Elizabeth's favourite."

He totters off on his big-buckled, high-heeled shoes into his bedroom.

We all watch him with our mouths hanging open.

"What's happened to Dad?" says Rupert.

"I think he got vain," I tell him. I'm surprised as well. I know Dad was a bit worried about losing his hair and getting close to fifty. It must be bothering him more than I thought.

Ryan trudges back to the garage. He just can't stop inventing. I suppose he's working on Dad's calf-expanders now.

I'm curious. So I ask Rupert, "What's this privy like then? Are you really going to take it to the Fayre?"

"Course we are," says Rupert. "We'll just load it in the back of the van. People will be really interested. I bet they've never seen a queen's personal privy before."

"But what's it look like?"

"Err," says Rupert, shuffling about and looking a bit shifty. "In the book it looks dead simple. There's just a big tank of water at the top—"

"You haven't actually seen it yet, have you?" I interrupt him.

"No," admits Rupert. "Ryan's keeping it secret until the big day. But he's given me the key."

Rupert holds up a large metal key.

"What are you talking about? Why do you need a key?"

"Ryan says Sir John Harrington had one. To unlock a little brass grille, so you could flush it out. Anyway, now I'm Keeper of the Key of the Queen's Privy," he says, as if that's more important. "Instead of just Keeper of the Queen's Privy. Right?"

He slips the key into his pocket. He seems really proud of it. "I told you Ryan wouldn't mess around with my privy. I told you he was making it just like that drawing in the history book."

But I'm still worried. I need to see Rebel. If there's nothing surprising about this privy, why is Ryan keeping it secret?

"Look," I ask Rupert, "are you sure you want to take this privy on Saturday? I've been doing some research. I've read about that flush toilet. Queen Elizabeth didn't even like it. She was scared to use it."

Rupert's really offended. "No!" he cries. "I don't believe it! Scared of my toilet? My toilet is a friendly little toilet. I love my toilet. Anyone would be thrilled to use it, even a queen."

"But you haven't even seen it," I say, through gritted teeth.

"You're just trying to spoil things, Rae! You're just jealous 'cos I'm Keeper of the Key of the Queen's Privy and you're not!"

He stomps off. Now I really, really need to see Rebel. Everyone around me seems to be going crazy. Dad fancies himself. Rupert's in love with a toilet. Ryan's got calf-expanders on the brain.

Even Mum says, when I go through the

kitchen, "Your dad looks handsome in that Elizabethan get-up, doesn't he? Quite romantic, really. He should wear it all the time."

Oh, no! Even Mum's joining in, getting all excited about the Elizabethans. I'm disgusted. She's not even in Rent-a-Rabble. But here she is, going all starry-eyed over Dad's costume. What's going on? You can usually rely on my mum to stay level-headed.

Our historical hound's in the garden, cocking his leg up against the trees. He's the only one I can tell my worries to. We sit on the back step together.

"Rebel," I ask him, anxiously, "you haven't gone Elizabethan-crazy have you?"

He just raises his eyebrows as if to say, "What? Are you joking? I'm a modern twenty-first century dog."

"Just checking," I tell him.

Then I make a confession. "You know I said I was never going to wear a—"

"*Ruff*," interrupts Rebel.

"No, not a ruff. A beard. I said I was never going to be a Bearded Lady at the Fayre?"

"*Ruff*."

"Well, I'm going to be. I'm going to have the biggest, bushiest false beard you've ever seen. Then at least none of my friends will recognize me!"

Chapter Six

It's the Elizabethan Fayre tomorrow but I still haven't made my beard. I can't get enthusiastic about it, somehow.

But Dad has made one for himself, to add to his Sir Walter Rabble costume. It hooks over his ears. He must have remembered what Rupert said about Sir Walter Raleigh's beard being attractive to ladies. Because

Dad's beard is turned up too. It flicks up at the end like a goblin's.

It looks ridiculous. But it's no good telling him. He's lost all common sense over that costume. He parades around in it all the time, admiring himself in mirrors.

Like I said before – it's the first time in his life my dad's ever been interested in fashion. Pity it's the fashion of four hundred years ago.

Even Rupert said, "Dad, that costume's a bit, well, sissy, isn't it?"

Dad was really hurt. "Your mum thinks it's romantic."

I've heard Dad practising his Elizabethan compliments on Mum. "Your lips are like cherries. Your teeth, no, I mean, your *eyes* are like stars!"

And Mum just giggles. I've never heard my mum giggle before. She's just not a giggly person. I even saw Dad kissing her hand. Honestly, your own parents carrying on like that. It's so embarrassing! And Rebel agrees with me. *"Ruff,"* he said, when I told him.

"I know it's rough, Rebel. I don't know any

other kids that have to put up with a family like mine."

We're having a rehearsal after tea. Usually Rent-a-Rabble is well prepared. We know what we're going to be, what we're going to do. But this Elizabethan job is different. Dad seems to have lost his grip. He seems to be floating around on a cloud half the time.

All he's worried about is his calves. His legs still look like white sticks.

"I might have to resort to bran after all," he tells me, turning sideways to look in the mirror. "Ryan still hasn't finished that calf-expander thing yet."

"Yes, I have," says Ryan, suddenly appearing in the doorway.

Dad's usually pretty suspicious about Ryan's inventions. He hates it when Ryan improves on history. But he seems really keen to try this one out. That's how much my dad's changed. Just by putting on that costume he's become a completely different person!

"What kind of contraption is that?" says Dad, when Ryan shows him a jumble of tubes and rubber bags. "It looks like something horrible they'd use in a hospital."

"I call it Calf Inflator," says Ryan, sounding really confident. "See these two air canisters? With long tubes attached to them and rubber bags at the end? Well, there's one for each leg. The canisters go inside your breeches, one on each hip."

Dad opens his mouth to interrupt. I'm sure he's going to say, "I can't use that, son. It's not authentic."

But instead he says, in an excited voice, "I get it! A tube goes down each leg. And a rubber bag sort of sits on each calf. Right?"

"Right!" says Ryan. "It's really simple. You just twist these valves, give each bag a few blasts of air. And, hey presto, Calf Inflator gives you big calves! And if your calves deflate, no sweat, you can just pump them up again! Without anyone knowing. It's a big improvement on bran, isn't it? You have total control!"

Dad's already fiddling about with his breeches, trying to cram in the Calf Inflator.

It's against the principles of Rent-a-Rabble, using modern inventions. I mean, did they have air canisters in Elizabethan times? I don't think so. But since Dad became Sir Walter Rabble he's chucked all those principles out of the window.

"Can you see it?" says Dad, anxiously checking the mirror.

"No," says Ryan. No one would guess Dad's wearing a secret Calf Inflator. It's all hidden away under his breeches.

"OK, Dad," says Ryan. "Are you ready? Pump up those calves!"

On Dad's right calf, under his tights, a swelling pops up.

"It's working!" says Ryan.

The swelling gets big as a grapefruit. But nothing's happening to Dad's left leg. It still looks like a twig. Hang on, there's a tiny, piddly bump coming up, like a kneecap in the wrong place.

"Dad, Dad," says Ryan, "give your left leg more air! You've got to inflate them both the same size. Or it looks really freaky!"

"I know," says Dad gazing in the mirror. "But it's not that easy to operate. It's going to take practice."

Dad looks really determined to get the

hang of it. He pumps in more air – lots more air.

"No, Dad, no," warns Ryan. "That's way too much! Your tights won't stand the strain!"

Dad's calves are the same size now. But they're as big as balloons. And getting bigger!

"Aaargh!" screams Rupert, who's just come in. "Aliens have taken over Dad's body. Look, they're hatching out of his legs!"

Trust Rupert to go over the top. Dad just looks to me like he's got two pillows stuffed down his tights.

"Don't get hysterical, Rupert. Dad's only inflating his calves."

"Stop, Dad!" warns Ryan. "Or your calves'll burst!" He sounds a bit panicky. It must be a dangerous situation because Ryan never sounds panicky.

Dad stops.

"Phew," says Ryan, wiping his forehead. "That was close. That's way too heavy on the air, Dad. You've got to have a lighter touch."

"Why, do you think they're too big?" asks Dad, checking the mirror again.

"They're grotesque, Dad," I have to be honest. "It looks like your legs are pregnant."

Dad doesn't want to believe me. He's thrilled to bits with his new calves.

"I think they look quite manly," he says. "Anyway, how big is big? What size calves did fashionable Elizabethan lords actually have? They might have been even bigger than this."

I don't know either. History books don't tell you useful things like that.

"I'll just go and ask your mother," decides Dad. "She's taken a lot of interest in my costume. We'll see what she says."

He hobbles off down the stairs holding on to the banister. It's hard to walk in high heels with manly calves. I don't know how those Elizabethan gallants managed it.

We all watch him go. Then we stare at each other. There's total silence for about ten seconds.

Rupert breaks it, of course. "I want my old scruffy Dad back," he says. "I don't like Sir Walter Rabble."

I know what he means. Rupert makes one

of his ghastly faces. I think it's the *"grisly corpse long buried"*. Then stomps off into his bedroom.

But there's another thing worrying me besides Dad.

"This toilet we're taking to the Fayre tomorrow," I ask Ryan, "is it authentic? I mean, is it exactly the same as the Elizabethan one?"

Ryan looks shifty. "Err, not exactly," he admits.

"So, what's different about it?"

Usually Ryan doesn't say much. He's on another planet most of the time. But when he starts talking about his inventions he's like Rupert. You can't shut him up.

"You know those new Japanese toilets? Remember we saw them on that telly programme?"

"I don't remember that."

"Well, they're toilets especially built to reduce stress. They play you soothing music and warm water jets massage your bottom. And they've got a heated seat and everything. They even talk to you. When tiny little kids are just learning to use the toilet, a voice says, 'Well done. Brilliant shot!'"

"A talking toilet?" Dreadful suspicions are springing up in my brain.

"So, I thought it must have been dead stressful being Queen Elizabeth. I mean, the court was full of plots and traitors. She was always having to chop people's heads off. So I've just added a few improvements. To make her privy really relaxing."

"But it isn't authentic, Ryan. Elizabethans didn't have talking toilets. Remember, Rent-a-Rabble always tells it like it was."

I don't know why that's important. Dad doesn't seem to think it's important these days.

Ryan can't see the problem. "I know," he says. "But they would have had toilets like that if they'd had the technology."

"Have you told Rupert about this?"

Ryan looks even more shifty.

"Err, not yet," he says. "I thought it would be a big surprise."

"You're not kidding."

A terrible feeling of doom is sweeping over me. What's going on? Rent-a-Rabble seems to be falling apart. And Dad's just letting it happen.

"I'm going now," I tell Ryan. "I've got something I need to do."

He looks after me, puzzled.

"What do you need to do, Rae?"

"I need to make myself a beard for tomorrow. A very, very big beard."

Chapter Seven

Mum's gone off to meet her important Japanese clients at the airport. She's got her smart, black business suit on. "We're having a working lunch, then we're coming straight to the Elizabethan Fayre," she says. "So I'll see you this afternoon."

She thinks Rent-a-Rabble is all prepared. I think she's in for a big shock.

Am I the only one who's worrying? Dad doesn't seem worried at all. I have to go upstairs to prise him away from the mirror.

He says, "Do you think this extra plume on my cap is a bit over the top?"

He's all dressed up as Sir Walter Rabble with the Calf Inflator hidden inside his costume. At least his legs aren't bulging too badly. Mum must have had a word. He's let them down to a sensible size. Now his calves look like a weight lifter's. Pity the rest of him is like a string bean.

It's breezy outside. A gust of wind catches Dad's enormous ruff. It blows up and all that white frilly stuff wraps round his head.

Dad staggers about in circles. "Help! My ruff's blinding me!"

Rebel and me raise our eyebrows at each other. "What's that madman doing now?" Rebel would say if he could speak. Dad stumbles backwards into a tree. But it doesn't hurt him. His cushiony calves act like car bumpers and bounce him off again. He wrestles with his ruff and rips it off his face.

"Phew! I've just had an authentic

Elizabethan experience!" gasps Dad. He sounds really thrilled. "I read about it in a history book. That was the big problem with ruffs. They flapped in your face on windy days. I bet those extra-starchy ones could knock you out cold!"

"Hi, Dad!" says Rupert. He and Ryan are busy loading Queen Elizabeth's privy into the van. They don't seem worried either.

"Don't you go making faces at babies!" I warn Rupert. Then I remember something else. "You haven't got that straw with you, have you?"

"No, I've lost it somewhere."

That's one less thing to worry about.

The privy looks like a load of old scrap. All I can recognize is a sort of water tank on the top and a box thing where you sit and a tangle of metal pipes. I wouldn't be seen dead sitting on that heap of junk. Especially if I was a queen.

Dad says, "You won't let anyone use it, will you, Rupert? That wouldn't be hygienic. It's not connected to the drains."

"Course not," says Rupert, shocked. "It's strictly reserved for the bum of good Queen

Bess. Just anyone can't use it. I'll make sure of that. Besides, I've got the key."

He waves the key importantly around.

Rupert's dressed himself in a really weird outfit. He's got a scratchy, brown woollen jerkin from our costume cupboard. That's OK. That's the kind of thing Rent-a-Rabble usually wears. But he's decorated it with gold braid and silver fringes and a row of shiny medals. He looks like a walking Christmas tree! He swears it's authentic. That it's the official uniform of the Keeper of the Key of the Queen's Privy. But I think that's a load of old rubbish. He made it all up. He's taking advantage of the fact that Dad's lost the plot.

For the first time since he became Sir Walter Rabble, Dad looks uneasy. Like there are some things that might have slipped his mind. "How does this royal privy actually work?" he asks.

"Oh, Ryan knows all that," says Rupert. "He's going to be there to explain it. Don't you worry, Dad, we've got it all under control."

"And what are you and our historical hound going to be, Rae?"

It's a bit late to be asking that. Dad should have sorted all this out ages ago. It's a good job I haven't lost my grip.

"I'm going to be a Bearded Lady and Rebel here is going to be a Bearded Lady's dog."

"*Ruff*," says Rebel. He sounds fed up.

Dad opens his mouth to ask another question. But he can see by the expression on our faces that neither of us is in a good mood.

"Let's go then, fellow members of Rent-a-Rabble."

We all pile into our old blue van.

"I'll have to deflate my calves a bit to drive," says Dad.

A tiny, squeaky raspberry sound fills the air.

"Where did that come from? Rupert, was that you?"

"Wasn't me," shrugs Rupert, looking wide-eyed and innocent.

"Yes, it was. It's always you. And you always blame somebody else."

We hit the road.

"Dad! Dad!" shouts Rupert, loud enough to make the van windows rattle.

"What Rae says is rubbish, isn't it? You don't think Queen Elizabeth would be scared of my privy?"

"Course not, son," says Dad vaguely. But he's not really listening. He's busy adjusting the extra plumes on his hat in the driving mirror.

Chapter Eight

"I say, will someone from Rent-a-Rabble please shift their dirty old van," demands a loud, snooty voice. "It's hardly Elizabethan, is it?"

I don't even have to turn round. I know who that is. It's Nigel's mum giving orders. She just loves being in charge.

"What does she know about being

Elizabethan?" I'm thinking. She isn't a history expert like my dad.

"Hurry, hurry!" says Nigel's mum. "The Fayre will be opening in half an hour."

"Sorry," says Dad. "We've only just arrived. I'll move it in a second. We're just unloading our stuff."

"Don't apologize to her, Dad!" I hiss at him. "She's just like Nigel. She thinks she's better than everyone else. She hasn't got the right to boss us around."

"Yes, she has," says Dad. "She is Queen Elizabeth, after all."

I turn round. "Oh, no."

Nigel's mum has got the biggest costume I've ever seen! Trust her. She's padded up like an American footballer. Her skirt makes her look two metres wide. She's taking up enough space for ten people! Dad looks weedy beside her, even with his inflated calves.

"Look at her frock!" gasps Rupert. "It could stand up all on it own. You could use it as a circus big top!"

"Big frocks were all the rage in Elizabethan times," says Dad. "And, of

76

course, Queen Elizabeth's would be bigger than anyone else's. I'm guessing she's got whalebone hoops under that skirt to make it stick out. Magnificent sight, isn't she?"

Her Majesty comes gliding towards us. You can't see her feet moving under that big skirt. It's like she's on skates. She knocks several people over and doesn't even notice. Her dress is all glittery with pearls and jewels. It's like a carnival costume. You need shades to look at it!

I bet she hired that, I'm thinking, *from some posh costume shop. That's not fair. Rent-a-Rabble makes all their own stuff.*

She's not authentic either. Even if she is wearing whalebones. Queen Elizabeth didn't look like that. She had rotten teeth and a red wig. Her face was painted with white lead and her cheeks with red dye. She must have looked like a clown!

I'm just about to say, "Why aren't your teeth black?" when, I can't believe it, Dad makes a bow. He'd better not expect me to curtsey.

"Sir Walter Rabble at your service, Your Majesty."

If he thinks she's going to admire his manly calves he's in for a big disappointment. She just sweeps him aside. She's seen someone more important. "Ah, Lady Mayoress, welcome!"

"That woman!" I tell Ryan. "Who does she think she is?"

"Don't you know? That's Queen Elizabeth herself," says Rupert, in an awed voice. "She's come to visit her personal privy. I told you she wasn't scared of it. Here's the key, Your Majesty!" He sounds really excited.

"We haven't unloaded her privy yet," Ryan reminds him. But Queen Elizabeth wasn't listening anyway. She whacks Rupert out the way with her whalebone skirts. Then sails down to the car park.

"I bet she comes back later," says Rupert, staggering to his feet. His eyes are all dreamy. I think he's star-struck. He's never met a queen before.

"She's coming back already."

Someone yells, "Mind your backs!" Rupert stands to attention and salutes. Dad does another bow. But Queen Elizabeth doesn't give us a glance. Not even a haughty one. She just ignores us as if we're worms.

"What's that she's carrying?" I ask Ryan. She didn't have it before. She must have got it out of her car.

"Don't ask me," says Ryan. "Is it alive? It looks like a long-haired rat."

"It's a lap dog," Dad corrects him. "That's a nice authentic detail! Lap dogs were very popular at the Elizabethan Court. Ladies often carried them around. They led very pampered lives. They had their own velvet cushions. They were fed on the finest foods. Like roast chicken."

"*Ruff?*" Rebel pokes his nose out the back of the van. He seems suddenly interested.

"You can't be a lap dog," I tell him. "So don't even think about it. You don't look right. You're not a goggle-eyed, pea-brained floor mop. You're a proper dog!"

He still seems interested. He leaps out of the van and trots after Queen Elizabeth. His little legs are twinkling. He's in a hurry. His stumpy tail's wagging like mad. That's unusual. Rebel never wags his tail for humans. He's got too much pride for that.

"Where's Rebel going?" asks Rupert.

"Oh, dear," says Dad. "You know our Rebel's a bit of a Romeo? Well, don't look now, but I think he's fallen in love again."

"What, with that excuse for a pooch?" I thought Rebel had more taste.

"Remember that Great Dane he fell for?"

Rebel's got brains. But he's got one big weakness. When he's in love his brains turn to jelly. He completely loses his cool. His judgement goes right out the window.

He catches up with Queen Elizabeth. His tail's wagging so fast it's just a blur. He starts sniffing round her skirts. She doesn't notice him at first.

He barks, "*Ruff!*" She finally looks down and sees him.

Just at that moment, Rebel cocks his leg.

"Oh, no!" Dad cringes. He covers his eyes. He can't bear to look. "Rebel!" he screams. "Come here, boy!"

Rebel never comes when he's called. Not unless he wants to. And anyway, it's too late.

Queen Elizabeth goes completely nuts. "Whose is this filthy mongrel pestering my Precious? Look what he's done to my costume!"

She tries to swat Rebel away. But her dress won't let her bend down. And her skirt's so big he just sneaks round the other side of it. "Where's he gone?"

He's having another sniff.

"Get off! Get off!" shrieks Queen Elizabeth. "You disgusting creature!" She clutches Precious even tighter.

Rebel backs off. Or else her screams might burst his ear drums.

Her Majesty sweeps away.

Rebel waits a bit. Then he tippy-toes after her. She's not going to shake him off that easily. I might as well forget about him being a Bearded Lady's dog. He's got more important things on his mind.

"How could Rebel do that?" says Rupert. He's nearly lost for words. He's very upset. "That's – that's Queen Elizabeth!"

Attaboy, Rebel, I'm thinking. She'd better keep a close watch on Precious, her pedigree pooch. Rebel never gives up, not when he's got that really determined look in his eye.

Then I think of something else. Once she gets her skirt cleaned up, Queen Elizabeth is a sure bet to win that costume competition. Dad might as well not bother entering. And Rent-a-Rabble can kiss goodbye to that fifty pounds.

Chapter Nine

Rupert and Ryan are busy setting up the privy. It's hidden behind authentic willow-woven screens.

"I do hope Queen Elizabeth comes back to see it," says Rupert, clasping his hands like it's his dearest wish. "It would be a truly great honour. I know I'm only a humble Keeper of the Key of the Queen's

Privy. But I'm going to ask for her autograph!"

"Hmmm," says Dad. "But will people know what they're looking at? You ought to have had some explanatory notes. 'This is an exact replica of the flushing privy Sir John Harrington invented in 1592 for his godmother Queen Elizabeth.' Something like that."

Ryan gives a modest cough. "Actually, Dad, it's not an exact replica. It's got a bigger flush, for a start. And a few little extra features."

But Dad's not listening. The Fayre's open. The crowds are pouring in now. "Time to mingle with the public," says Dad. He gives his calves a few quick blasts of air.

"Don't overdo it, Dad!" Ryan reminds him.

Dad fluffs up his ruff. He juts out his chin. Sir Walter Rabble is ready to go.

"Are you coming, Rae? I'm off for a stroll round the Fayre."

"Errr, in a minute."

I haven't shown anyone my homemade beard yet. It's still inside the van. I'm a bit worried about it. I wanted it to be big enough to hide my face. But I got a bit carried away.

I put my beard on in the back of the van. I wish I had a mirror. It seems even bigger today, more wild and whiskery, as if it's grown like Jack's beanstalk overnight. I'm nearly tripping over it. And I seem to have overdone the moustaches. I can't see where I'm going. I have to make two spy holes to see through.

"What's that hairy thing supposed to be?" a kid says as I walk past.

That starts all his friends guessing.

"It's Chewbacca from *Star Wars*. It's Cousin It from *The Addams Family*."

"Don't be silly," a grown-up says. "It's an ancient breed of long-haired sheep."

No one guesses right. No one says, "Obviously, that's a Bearded Lady."

It just shows how ignorant people are about history. Sometimes I think it's hardly worth Rent-a-Rabble trying so hard to get the details right. What's the point, if no one knows how authentic you're being?

But it's a brilliant disguise. I can wander around where I like. There are some kids from my class over there. They look really puzzled when I walk by.

"It's a walking loo-brush!" someone says. They don't have a clue that it's me, Rae Rabble, inside.

The Fayre is packed with people. There are stalls everywhere, selling apples and ale and pies and lace.

There's a woman in Elizabethan costume. She's got a basket. She's crying, "Buy my fine cherries. What do you lack?"

It's all really cheery and jolly. There are musicians playing jigs on pipes and drums. There are pedlars and puppet shows and jugglers and wrestlers and tumblers. There's even a goose girl, with geese hissing and pecking all round her.

And Dad was right – there's a pig woman here. But she's not looking after pigs, like I thought. She's cooking them. There's a poor little sizzling piglet on a spit and she's hacking off bits and selling roast pork sand-wiches.

That's not Elizabethan, I'm thinking. *Sandwiches weren't invented until the eigh-teenth century.* And anyway, it's gross. I couldn't eat those sandwiches. That piglet would put me right off.

Who are those people all huddled together, whispering? The men are in grey suits. The Lady Mayoress is there with her golden chain. I sidle up to them in my hairy disguise.

They're having secret talks about the costume competition.

"There's only one choice really," someone says. "It's got to be a royal winner."

"Queen Elizabeth?"

"I think so, don't you? Her costume outshines everyone else's."

"And, of course," someone else reminds them, "the lady inside it did organize this whole event. And she's a very important person in the local community. So it's only fair. . ."

It's not fair. It's a fix! I'm thinking. *She doesn't need the prize money, not like Rent-a-Rabble do!*

"Mind you," says the Lady Mayoress. "There's an Elizabethan gentleman I've had my eye on. Have you seen him? What fine, manly calves. Quite outstanding!"

But none of the men in grey suits agree with her. I slink away. I need to find Dad, urgently.

There he is, strutting around as Sir Walter Rabble. I can see his purple plumes bobbing above the crowds.

I dodge between people to reach him.

"Dad!"

He's inflated his calves again. Ryan told him not to do that. No wonder the Lady Mayoress was impressed.

He's got a scented hanky from somewhere. He's holding to his nose. I know that's authentic. There were terrible stinks around in Elizabethan times. But it's not exactly tactful is it?

"Foh!" he's saying. "What foul stench is that?"

"You talking to me?" says a man in a vest with big muscles and lots of tattoos.

I rush in and rescue Dad before he gets thumped.

"Come on, Dad," I say, dragging him out of danger. He looks down, totally baffled.

"It's me, Dad."

"Oh, Rae, I didn't recognize you. Fantastic costume! Now, let me guess. You're some kind of yak from the Mongolian plains. Am I right?"

"A yak? What are you talking about?"

"Well, at some Fayres, they did put exotic wild beasts on display."

"I'm not a yak, Dad," I say, wearily. "I'm a Bearded Lady. Remember? I told you."

I'm sick of people getting it wrong. You'd think at least my own dad could get it right.

But there are more important things to discuss.

"Dad," I tell him, "the parade for the costume competition is at two o'clock. And you're going to lose. It's a big fix."

"I wonder if your mum is here yet?" says Dad, looking round. "How are my calves? They aren't fully inflated yet. Should I give them a few more puffs?"

"Concentrate, Dad! Forget about what you look like, for just two seconds."

But he's wandered off again, looking for Mum. Or maybe to find a mirror. It's no good depending on him. Becoming Sir Walter Rabble has turned his brain to scrambled egg.

And there's someone else over there who's let me down. It's Rebel.

As soon as I spot him, I think, "Oh no, we're in trouble."

It's no good calling to him. He's racing in the opposite direction. And there's a floor mop running beside him. It's Precious. What's Nigel's mum going to say when she finds out our mongrel, who came from a dogs' home, has run off with her pedigree pooch?

I answer my own question. "She's not going to be pleased, Rae."

They look happy though. They look wild and free. I bet Precious has never been wild and free in her life. Her silky blonde hair is blowing in the wind.

I can't help saying, "Awww, how sweet," as they disappear behind a stall selling gingerbread hearts.

Then Rupert nearly trips over me.

"Sorry, sorry, Mr Werewolf!"

"It's me – Rae – you idiot! I'm a Bearded Lady." I'm getting really tired of telling people that. "What are you doing here? You're supposed to be guarding the Queen's Privy."

"Ryan's looking after it for a minute."

Rupert seems in a strange mood. Excited and upset at the same time. He's jigging from one foot to the other. That means he's going to do something reckless.

"OK," I sigh. "Tell me what's going on."

"Gilbert's here! This Land Rover drove by. And he was in a trailer at the back."

"What's he doing here?"

"He's a historical pig, isn't he?" says Rupert still hopping about. "He gets hired out, just like us."

I ought to explain. When we were medieval peasants on our last job, Gilbert was in our hovel. He was playing our family pig. He's a sort of whale-pig actually – big and blubbery. He's covered with black spots. He doesn't do much. Just slobbers and snuffles in straw. But Rupert wanted to take him home. He was really sad when Dad got decisive, for once, and said, "Over your mum's dead body!"

"I've got to rescue him, right NOW!" says Rupert, frantically.

"What from?"

"From being roasted by that wicked pig lady. Have you seen what she's doing to pigs, Rae? It's horrible!"

"They won't roast Gilbert. He weighs about two tons for a start. They've just brought him here for people to look at."

But there's a tiny hint of doubt in my voice. Gilbert would make an awful lot of roast pork sandwiches.

"See, you're worried about him too," says Rupert. "Let's go and find him."

"All right." I think I've just made a big mistake. I'm too soft-hearted. I should have told Rupert, "You're on your own."

It's not hard to find Gilbert. You just follow your nose. He's rolling around in his pen, grunting. But his little piggy eyes are gleaming with intelligence. At least, Rupert says it's intelligence.

Rupert throws himself at his pig. "Gilbert! I thought I'd never see you again!" It's like he's greeting a long-lost friend.

"Are you sure this is a good idea?" I whisper, as Rupert grabs the rope round Gilbert's neck and unfastens the gate to his pen. "You're going to get very pongy."

"I don't mind that," says Rupert cheerily. "Privy keepers were pongy. It'll just make me more authentic."

Gilbert's well-trained. He trots obediently beside Rupert like a dog. A very big, wobbly, spotty dog.

"You know, Rupert," I say uneasily, "we shouldn't be taking him, really. I'm pretty sure they weren't going to roast him."

"But we can't be one hundred per cent sure, can we?" I think Rupert knows, as well as I do, that they wouldn't make Gilbert into butties. He just wants his company. "I really missed him," says Rupert, scratching Gilbert's bristly back.

"You've got to take him back at the end of the Fayre. Remember, Mum's coming this afternoon, with some VIP guests. We don't want to cause any trouble."

"Trouble?" says Rupert, as if he doesn't understand the word. "I'm going to be good as gold, honest, Rae." He leads Gilbert away.

I haven't got time to argue. I've seen Queen Elizabeth barging through the crowd like a battering ram. "Has anyone seen my Precious?"

And I've just had a brilliant idea.

Chapter Ten

I plant myself right in Queen Elizabeth's path. It's a bit risky. She could dazzle me with her jewels. Or whop me out of the way with those whalebone hoops. But she's so puzzled she stops dead. She looks down her frock at me.

"What are you supposed to be, may I ask?" she says, in that sneery voice that reminds me so much of Nigel's.

I'm sick of having to explain about the Bearded Lady.

"I'm a dancing bear," I tell her, jogging about a bit. "It's just not a very good costume."

"I can see that," says Queen Elizabeth, looking as if I'm a bad smell under her nose. I probably am a bad smell actually. I forgot that I've just been very close to Gilbert.

I'd better start grovelling. There's something I want Queenie to do. And I don't think it's going to be easy.

"Excuse me, Your Majesty, but would Your Majesty do us the great honour of paying a visit to her royal privy?"

"Royal privy?" snaps Nigel's mum suspiciously, dropping her posh voice. "What's all that about then?"

"Didn't you know there's one here for your own personal use? You can't expect the queen to share a privy with common people."

Queen Elizabeth looks flattered.

"Is this royal privy nice and roomy?" she asks me, being gracious again.

"Oh, yes, Your Majesty."

"Well, I'll come then," she says.

I can't believe it! Our luck must be changing. It wasn't as hard as I thought.

"There's a queue of rather common-looking people at the Portaloos," she explains. "And anyway, my dress won't go through the door. By the way," she says, suddenly fixing me with a glinty eye, "have you by any chance seen my Precious? Some scruffy mongrel was sniffing round her."

"What, me?" I say, using Rupert's wide-eyed innocent look. "Don't ask me. I can't see a thing in this dancing bear suit."

When Rupert sees the queen approaching he nearly faints with happiness.

"I knew she'd come," he whispers to Ryan. "What an honour!"

"What are you supposed to be?" snaps Good Queen Bess. She's hopping from one foot to another. She seems to be getting very impatient about something.

"I'm your humble servant, Your Majesty!" yells Rupert, in his boomiest voice. "I'm the Keeper of the Key of the Queen's Privy!"

He waves the key in front of her face. Than he makes a little speech in praise of his toilet.

"Before you enter, your Majesty," roars Rupert, "allow me to tell you about this flushing privy. It was built by my hero, Sir John Harrington. He was a genius and knew loads of rude jokes. But everyone made fun of his invention. That usually happens to geniuses! Look at my brother, Ryan—"

"Yes, yes, yes! Never mind all that rubbish!" shouts Queen Elizabeth rudely. She snatches the key from him. "Just let me in there. I'm desperate." She rushes behind the willow screens.

A moment later a frantic voice comes from inside.

"How do you work this thing?"

"Tell the queen what to do, Ryan," orders Rupert.

Ryan moves closer to the willow screens and begins to shout instructions through it. They sound very complicated. Unlock this, press that, turn that valve. "I should have written a manual," he says.

From inside the willow screens comes a strange gurgling sound. Then a terrible clanking starts up.

"I hope she hasn't got the heated-seat button mixed up with the bottom massager," murmurs Ryan to himself.

He yells through the screens, "Just relax, Your Majesty. Prepare to be pampered by your privy!"

"*Oink, Oink!*"

I flash a horrified look at Rupert. "You didn't!"

"It's not my fault. Where was I supposed to hide him?"

A strangled scream comes from inside.

"There's a pig in here!"

"Don't panic!" Rupert reassures her. "It's only Gilbert."

The willow screens start to shake. The clanking sound gets louder, fiercer. What's going on in there?

"This toilet's gone mad! Help! Help! Get me out of here."

"Oh, dear," says Ryan. "I think it needs a few adjustments!" he shouts helpfully through the screens.

The screens are wobbling like mad! The privy's out of control!

"Good shot!" yaks a weird, robot voice.

"Well done, good shot, well done, good shot, well done, good shot," over and over again like Rupert singing a madrigal.

"Get me out of here! This thing's alive!" That's Queen Elizabeth yelling.

Gilbert rushes out squealing. He disappears in the crowd. Rupert runs after him. "Gilbert! Wait for me!"

The screens won't stop shuddering. *Clank!* "Good shot!" *Whoosh!*

"What's that waterfall sound?"

Ryan shrugs apologetically. "It's the extra-powerful flush."

"Do something to stop it!"

"I can't. It's a smart toilet. It's got a mind of its own."

"Oh, great! Now you tell me."

It sounds like Niagara Falls in there. Water's pouring out under the screens. They give one extra big wobble, then fall flat.

"Oh, no." Water's flooding round my feet.

It's a disaster area! The toilet was like a piece of junk before. Now it looks like an exploded piece of junk in a puddle. "Well done, good shot, well. . ." a mechanical voice from somewhere is saying in a strange, slow growl. It slows down even more. "Well . . . done . . . good. . ." Then stops.

"It's fallen apart under the strain," says Ryan, shaking his head sadly. "I just asked it to do too much. It got confused."

Queen Elizabeth is sitting next to the wreck of her personal privy. Her gorgeous dress is in ruins.

"Where am I?" she's asking, in a dazed voice, trying to cram her waterlogged wig back on her head.

I didn't mean for this to happen. I had a weedy plan. I just wanted Rupert to keep her talking so she missed the costume competition.

But I can't help thinking, *Wow! This plan is so much better.*

You'd almost think that privy was on our side. That it knew exactly what it was doing.

"Don't be stupid, Rae!" I scold myself. "Toilets don't have brains!" No matter what Ryan says.

Dad was right about how water ruins ruffs. Queen Elizabeth's has gone all floppy. She staggers to her feet. She sounds really squelchy. Every time she moves she squirts water. That padded frock has soaked it up like a sponge.

"Look at the state of my gown!" she rages, dripping water everywhere. "It's soaking! You idiots! Just wait until I've wrung myself out."

She takes a good squint at me. "Wait a minute!" she says. "Don't I know you?"

How can she? I'm in disguise. Then I put a hand to my face. It feels smooth and not hairy. In all the excitement my beard's fallen off.

"You're in my Nigel's class, aren't you? You're one of those pesky Rabbles. Well, you're going to regret this. I'm going to make sure that you lot never, ever work again!"

She hobbles furiously away. She can hardly walk. That soggy frock must weigh a ton.

"Ryan," I say, "we're in big trouble now. Nigel's mum knows the Lady Mayoress. She knows everyone."

She isn't making empty threats. She really could ruin Rent-a-Rabble.

But Ryan's not listening. He's already scribbling diagrams on his hand, inventing an even better privy. "I think I made the flush too powerful," he's muttering to himself.

"You don't have to be a genius inventor to see that! Even I could see that!"

But it's no good using my sarcastic voice. He's in a world of his own, where I can't reach him. He wanders off, still muttering.

There's an announcement over the loudspeaker.

"Will everyone entering the costume competition please come to the prizegiving platform."

I'd better go. Mum will be there with her VIP guests. And, without Queen Elizabeth, Dad will probably win. But what good is that? We might as well pack up and go home. Rent-a-Rabble is finished.

Chapter Eleven

I go trudging though the crowds. I didn't
realize this Elizabethan Fayre was such a
swish event. There are lots of VIPs sitting in
rows on a platform. And local telly is here!
They're filming the whole thing.

There's Mum on the platform.

I give her a wave, "Hi, Mum!" She doesn't
wave back. Then I remember that I've put my

beard back on. There are two serious-looking men in smart grey suits sitting next to her. They must be her Japanese clients. They look a bit bewildered, as if they don't know what on earth's going on.

The Lady Mayoress is at the front, standing behind a microphone. It gives a tinny crackle. Then she coughs. "Can you hear me? Are all the entrants for the costume competition up here on the platform?"

She seems to be scanning the crowd. I bet she's looking for Queen Elizabeth. She doesn't know that Queen Elizabeth is drying herself out after the Attack of the Talking Toilet. That's upset their little plans. Now they're going to have to pick another winner. She has an urgent discussion with some people sitting on the front row.

But Dad's not there either. What's he playing at? He doesn't know Queen Elizabeth won't be entering. He probably thinks he doesn't stand a chance.

I look around quickly. There he is! You can't mistake those purple plumes. I rush through the crowd and grab him. "Dad!"

I'm not going to tell him yet what Nigel's

mum said about ruining Rent-a-Rabble. That would be too cruel. After all, this is Dad's big chance. He might even get on telly.

"Dad! Queen Elizabeth isn't in the costume competition. Go on, Dad, get up there. I bet Sir Walter Rabble will win."

Dad checks the platform. There's the goose girl up there, with some hissing geese. And a couple of minstrels with lutes and a guy with a bowling ball who's supposed to be Sir Francis Drake.

"You're right, Rae!" says Dad. He sounds really encouraged. "There's no one up there with calves like mine!"

He feels inside his breeches, finds the hidden air canisters and gives his calves a few quick blasts. "I wish I had a mirror," he frets.

"Dad, get up there! You look all right, honest. You look great."

"Do I?" says Dad. "Really? You're not just saying that?"

"Be proud, Dad. Remember you're Sir Walter Rabble!"

I push him towards the platform. He totters up the steps. He still hasn't got the hang of those high-heeled buckled shoes. He gives Mum a quick wave. She waves back. She says something to her Japanese clients. She's probably explaining, "That man in the ruff, that's my husband!" They look more glum and confused than ever. I don't think they're having a very good time. Mum'll be worried about that. She wanted to make a good impression.

The Lady Mayoress comes back to the microphone.

"With great difficulty, the judges have decided on a winner. And the winner is," she waves Dad forward, "Sir Walter Rabble!"

There's a massive burst of applause. The geese get all upset. They stretch out their necks, start hissing and pecking at anything near. And the nearest things just happen to be my Dad's inflatable calves. Dad tries to skip out of the way: "Shoo! Shoo!" he says. But they get in a couple of really good pecks.

"Oh no!" I cover my ears, screw my eyes tight shut. I'm expecting a big bang. I feel like shouting, "Take cover!"

Nothing happens. I can't understand it. Those rubber bags must be punctured. If they didn't explode, why aren't they deflating? Maybe Ryan built in some kind of safety device.

The applause dies down. I dare to open my eyes. The panic's over. The goose girl has driven her geese off the stage. And my dad, the winner, is standing by the Lady Mayoress at the microphone. I thought she'd give him a cheque. But she hands him a large clinking leather purse. Very Elizabethan. It must have the prize money inside it.

Dad accepts graciously. He does a low bow. Then he sees the TV cameras are on him. He adjusts his ruff, sweeps back his plumes and taps the mike. "Ahem, errr, can you hear me out there?"

Oh, no! My dithery dad's going to make a speech. In front of all these people! Thank goodness I'm in disguise.

But I needn't have worried. Dressed as Sir Walter Rabble, Dad's a different person. He's suave and dashing and confident. He doesn't waffle once! The Lady Mayoress is going weak at the knees. He's taking the chance to plug Rent-a-Rabble. Good job he doesn't know yet that it's probably the end of the road.

"Ladies and gentlemen," he says, "I am the Managing Director of Rent-a-Rabble, a new and thrusting enterprise. History is our Business! So if any of you good people are planning a historical event, give us a ring on –"

Dad just has time to tell them our telephone number when there's a rude raspberry sound. The kind Rupert makes when he wants to be gross and get on your nerves. Only this one's even louder. The mike broadcasts it all over the Fayre.

Dad looks in shocked surprise at the Lady Mayoress.

There goes another one. *PARP!* This time it really lets rip. It seems to go on for ever.

Two other things happen. Next to Mum, the Japanese business men start giggling. Soon they're shaking with laughter, trying to cover their mouths. And Queen Elizabeth staggers on to the stage, still dripping. She elbows the Lady Mayoress out of the way. "Am I too late for the costume competition?" she says.

There's just her and Dad at the mike. Another terrible trumping noise fills the fayre ground. It's loud as a rumble of thunder. Then another. And another. The Japanese businessmen have fallen off their chairs. They're rolling around on the floor clutching their bellies. They're pointing at Dad. But they're laughing so hard they can't speak.

Then I realize what's making the rude noise. It's not the Lady Mayoress. Or Queen Elizabeth. It's my dad's deflating calves.

That's it, then, I'm thinking, grimly. Dad's wrecked the dignity of the occasion. And it's all being filmed for the telly! Nigel's mum doesn't need to ruin Rent-a-Rabble. Dad's antics this afternoon have done the job for her.

TRRRUMP!

I can't stand any more of this. But no one seems to know how to stop it. The town's VIPs are looking really threatening. Mum's Japanese clients are still having hysterics. And Queen Elizabeth looks suddenly horrified. She's seen the cameras. She's realized she's on telly! She turns round, desperate to escape. But she's in the spotlight now. She's

in charge of all this. So she's got to do something to save the situation.

Then Dad grabs the mike. I can't believe it. What's he going to do now? What can he do?

There's one last, juicy, *Parp!* Then everything goes quiet. Dad's calves are flat as pancakes. He clears his throat. I'm cringing already. I'm thinking, *He's only going to make things worse.* But I should have had faith!

Dad's brilliant. He makes his speech in a cool, clear voice. "Ladies and gentlemen, what you are witnessing here is an authentic historical re-enactment. We tell it like it was, warts and all! Here's the story. One day, at Court, the Earl of Oxford was presented to Queen Elizabeth. He made a low bow to Her Majesty. And accidentally, at the same time, let loose a very impolite sound. The poor earl was so embarrassed that he sent himself into exile. Seven years later, when he thought no one could possibly remember, he returned. He was presented again to Queen Elizabeth. She smiled graciously upon him and spoke. 'My lord,' she said, 'I had forgot the fart.'"

Dad said a rude word, but it must be all right if Queen Elizabeth said it. There's silence for about two seconds. Then suddenly someone starts laughing. Phew! Soon everyone is laughing and clapping like mad. Even the angry Councillors and VIPs on the stage. Even the Lady Mayoress. The only people who aren't laughing are Mum's Japanese clients. They can't. They've already laughed so much that their stomachs are sore.

Ryan's standing next to me. Where'd he come from? I've got a few words to say to him.

"Ryan! Dad only got out of that by the skin of his teeth! You made Dad's inflatable calves out of whoopee cushions didn't you? What did you do that for?"

Ryan shrugs vaguely. "Is that what they were? They were just perfect for the job. They were lying around in Rupert's bedroom. . ."

I can't tell him off any more. It was very nearly a disaster. But, thanks to Dad's quick thinking, it's turned out to be a triumph.

Nigel's mum suddenly changes her mind

about Rent-a-Rabble. She sees that we're really popular. We're the stars of the show. So she decides to become our best friend. She pushes Dad aside and says, smiling into the TV camera, "Another round of applause for Rent-a-Rabble. I've always been one of their biggest fans."

What a cheek!

But I don't really mind. I can't be too mad. Because Dad's face, beaming with smiles when he hears all the clapping, makes up for anything.

Chapter Twelve

There was a sad parting between Gilbert and Rupert. It was really touching. Rupert was sniffing away, wiping his nose on his cuff. And I even thought I saw a tear sparkling in Gilbert's eye.

"Never mind," Dad told Rupert. "You're bound to meet him again at the next job."

"I know," sniffed Rupert, looking all tragic,

as Gilbert was loaded into his trailer. "But we always seem to be saying goodbye."

Nigel's mum was still looking for Precious when we left the Fayre. Rebel was missing, too. I saw them both, from the van window on the way home. It was getting dark by that time. We all saw them, silhouetted against the moon on a dark hill-top. They were side by side, staring into a starry sky.

Dad said, "We should go back, tell Nigel's mum where Precious is."

He didn't sound too keen. He was quite relieved when we outvoted him.

"No way!" Rupert, Ryan and me said, almost as one person.

Then I added, "Awwww, Dad, they look really happy. You can't tell on them."

Even Ryan said, "No, Dad. Let them have some private time together. It might be true love." I didn't know Ryan even thought about things like that.

"I suppose it's OK," said Dad. "They'll come back when they're ready, won't they? And Rebel will look after her."

He'd better. I don't think Precious is a very streetwise dog.

When we got home, Mum's car was parked in the drive. She was thrilled to bits. "My Japanese clients had a wonderful time," she told us. "They said they always thought British people had no sense of humour. But today has proved them wrong. And guess what, they've given my firm all their business!"

It's Monday night now. And we're all crowded round the telly, waiting for the local news. Dad has taken off his Sir Walter Rabble costume. He's back in his baggy jumper and saggy corduroy trousers.

"We might not be on," says Dad, anxiously. "You never know with TV. They cut you out if something more important happens."

But nothing more important has happened.

"That's Dad!" shrieks Rupert, as the TV announcer introduces the film about the Elizabethan Fayre. "Dad, Dad, you're on telly!"

They missed out the rude raspberries made by Dad's deflating calves. And the story about the Earl of Oxford. But they kept in the last bit where Nigel's mum said she was a big fan of Rent-a-Rabble.

I just hope none of my friends are watching. Having your dad on telly is cool. But having your dad on telly in high-heeled shoes wearing a big ruff, with whoopee cushions stuffed down his tights? Thank goodness he was only on for about three seconds. Blink, and you missed him. I'm just keeping my fingers crossed that nobody noticed.

"It's just a pity that prize wasn't real money," sighs Dad.

"That was a big cheat!" I say, disgusted. "Talk about mean! They should have said the prize was fifty fake gold sovereigns. Then you needn't have got dressed up in that daft costume."

Dad looks a bit hurt. Mum says, "I thought it really suited him."

Then Dad admits, in a serious voice. "Actually, you're right, Rae. That fake money was a warning to me. I shall never, ever, betray the principles of Rent-a-Rabble again by pretending to be a lord. No, it's serfs, swineherds, scullions and servants for me from now on. I'm pretty ashamed of myself, I don't mind telling you. I can't think what came over me."

"Oh, cheer up!" says Mum, briskly. "You got some brilliant publicity out of it. The name of your business mentioned on prime-time telly!" She does some quick sums on her calculator. "That's worth a fortune."

"Mum's right," agrees Dad. "That was a real piece of good luck. You know, kids, I truly believe Rent-a-Rabble is on the road to success. People will be queuing up to offer us work."

Rupert agrees with Dad, of course. He punches the air with his fist. "Yay! We've got it made, Dad. We're gonna be millionaires!"

Excuse me if I don't punch the air with him. I don't mean to be a party-pooper. But this good luck is spooky. It isn't what Rent-a-Rabble is used to. What if it doesn't last?

And excuse me if I don't throw my false beard in the bin just yet. I'm going to keep it handy in my bedroom. Because, you never know, I might need a good disguise again, one of these days.

Toffs and Toshers

"Guess what, kids? We've got our next job!"

Dad's just come bouncing into the kitchen. He's waving a letter about. And he's beaming all over his face.

"Oh, yeah?" I don't want to be a party-pooper. But I've only just recovered from our last job. It takes a long time to live down being an Elizabethan Bearded Lady.

"You know that Victorian street scene they've built right inside the City Museum?" asks Dad. "That's got shops and houses just like the real thing? Well, they're going to fill it with a big crowd of Victorian characters just for one day. And, guess what, they've hired us to be part of it."

"Cool!" shouts my little brother, Rupert. "Can we choose which Victorian characters we're going to be, Dad?"

"*Err*, within limits, son."

Why does Rupert even bother asking? He knows the rules. He knows we can't choose to be anyone important or powerful. You only have to look at the new snappy slogan that's painted on our van: "WE NEVER PLAY PRINCES. WE ARE PROUD TO PLAY PEASANTS AND PAUPERS!"

In case you haven't heard of us, we're Rent-a-Rabble, the real history people. You can look us up on our web site. We hire ourselves out for historical events. But we only ever play poor downtrodden people like serfs or servants or slaves.

"And, of course, we'll have to do some research," Dad replies to Rupert. "To make sure we're absolutely authentic. We must get the details right."

Dad's painted that on our van, too: "THE DRAMA'S IN THE DETAIL".

When our van passes by, people read our slogans, scratch their heads and say, *"What's that all about, then?"*

"But trust me," Dad rambles on, "you'll be spoiled for choice. The streets were swarming with poor, hungry, homeless people in Victorian times. People who shuffled around barefoot in rags and lived crowded into damp, stinking hovels."

"Wait a minute," I interrupt him. "That sounds familiar. Isn't that just like the peasants we played in our medieval job?"

But Dad doesn't get sarcasm; he never jokes about history.

"That's a very wise observation, Rae," he tells me, nodding gravely. "It's hundreds of years later. But poor people's lives haven't changed much."

So we're wearing brown rags again. Can't we wear shoes just once?

But I feel selfish and heartless when Dad cries, "Yes, they are still suffering!"

"Still suffering, Dad," repeats Rupert, like a parrot. Rupert can be such a creep.

Dad's getting on his soapbox now. "And Rent-a-Rabble are *privileged* to play The People Who Time Forgot. We Tell It Like It Was! Would you believe it, kids? Some of those poor wretches in Victorian times were reduced to collecting dog dirt! It was used in the tanning industry to darken leather. And they only got a penny a sack!"

"Did they, Dad?" says Rupert, his eyes

gleaming. Rupert loves anything disgusting. "Did they really collect dog dirt? Can I be a dog dirt collector, Dad? Can I? Can I? Do I need a shovel?"